The Colour Out of Space

*Lovecraft's Legendary Cosmic Horror
Tale –
Alien Forces Unleashed*

A Modern Translation

Adapted for the Contemporary Reader

H.P. Lovecraft

Translated by Tim Zengerink

Table of Contents

Preface - Message to the Reader

What If You Could Help Rebuild the Greatest Library in Human History?

Thousands of years ago, the Library of Alexandria stood as the crown jewel of human achievement — a sanctuary where the collected wisdom of every known civilization was gathered, preserved, and shared freely.

And then, it was lost.

Through fire, conquest, and the slow erosion of time, humanity lost not just books — but ideas, dreams, discoveries, and stories that could have changed the world forever.

Today, the Library of Alexandria lives again — and you are invited to be a part of its restoration.

Our mission is simple yet profound:

To rebuild the greatest library the world has ever known, and to translate all timeless works into every language and dialect, so that no seeker of knowledge is ever left behind again.

By joining our movement to rebuild the modern Library of Alexandria, you become part of an unprecedented mission:

- **Unlimited Access to the Greatest Audiobooks & eBooks Ever Written:**

  Instantly explore thousands of legendary works—Plato, Shakespeare, Jane Austen, Leo Tolstoy, and countless more. All instantly available to read or listen, placing a complete literary universe at your fingertips.

- **Beautiful Paperback & Deluxe Editions at Printing Cost**

  Own any title as an elegant paperback, deluxe hardcover, or stunning collectible boxset—offered to you at true printing cost, delivered straight to your door. Build your personal Library of Alexandria, crafted for beauty, built for durability, and worthy of proud display.

- **Fresh Translations for Modern Readers—in Every Language & Dialect**

  Enjoy timeless masterpieces reimagined in clear, contemporary language—no more outdated phrases or obscure references. Alongside the original versions, we're tirelessly translating these classics into every language and dialect imaginable, ensuring accessibility and understanding across cultures and generations.

- **Join a Global Renaissance of Literature & Knowledge**

  You directly support expanding our library, publishing deluxe editions at true cost, translating works into all global languages, and bringing humanity's greatest stories to people everywhere. By joining today, you're not just preserving a legacy of masterpieces; you set in motion a powerful wave of literary accessibility.

Become a Torchbearer of Knowledge.

Join us for free now at **LibraryofAlexandria.com**

Together, we will ensure that the light of human wisdom never fades again.

With gratitude and a shared love of knowledge,

The Modern Library of Alexandria Team

Visit:

www.libraryofalexandria.com

Or scan the code below:

Introduction

Beyond Human Comprehension: Lovecraft's Cosmic Vision

Among all of H.P. Lovecraft's influential works, The Colour Out of Space stands as a singular achievement—haunting, otherworldly, and profoundly unsettling. First published in 1927 in Amazing Stories, this short story marked a turning point in Lovecraft's creative evolution. It was his own favorite of all his tales, and for good reason: it crystallized the core of his unique vision, one that diverged sharply from traditional Gothic horror and lurched instead into a new genre he would come to define—cosmic horror.

What makes The Colour Out of Space so important, so terrifying, and so enduring is that it represents a different kind of fear—one not grounded in monsters or moral transgressions, but in the terrifying indifference of the universe. Lovecraft was not interested in ghosts or devils. Instead, he was preoccupied with what lies beyond the limits of human understanding. He asked: What if reality itself is stranger, darker, and more alien than anything our minds can process? What if the universe doesn't care about us at all?

In The Colour Out of Space, these questions find their purest and most devastating expression. The plot is deceptively simple: a meteorite crashes on a remote farm in the New England countryside, bringing with it a color—an actual color—that does not exist in the known spectrum. Over time, the land, the crops, the animals, and even the people on the farm begin to change. They decay, mutate, and lose their minds. The "colour" begins to seep into the earth and water, spreading its unearthly influence. But no one can quite describe what it is. No one can stop it. It is not evil in any traditional sense—it is simply beyond comprehension.

This is the essence of Lovecraftian horror. It's not a struggle between good and evil, but between human understanding and the vast, cold unknown. In Lovecraft's universe, the horror is not that something will come to kill us—it's that we were never important in the first place. The Colour Out of Space captures this sense of existential dread better than any other story in his oeuvre.

The story also signals Lovecraft's departure from his earlier, more derivative Gothic tales and toward a new, uniquely modern voice. Gone are the crumbling castles and brooding vampires. In their place, we find an unnamed surveyor investigating the site of a future reservoir in the Massachusetts countryside—an ordinary man who hears an extraordinary and disturbing story from an old local, Ammi Pierce. The framing device—a story within a story—adds to the tension and ambiguity, enhancing the sense that we are only ever hearing an interpretation of events that were themselves only partially understood.

Even the choice of language reflects Lovecraft's thematic intention. His characters struggle to describe what they see. The "colour" is something for which they have no words. This linguistic failure is not a flaw but a feature of the horror: it reinforces the idea that the universe contains realities our minds are not equipped to grasp. In a Lovecraftian world, horror arises from epistemological collapse—when the act of understanding itself begins to break down.

Science, Madness, and Environmental Decay

One of the most interesting aspects of The Colour Out of Space is its grounding in the real world. Set in the fictional "blasted heath" west of Arkham, the story draws heavily from the landscape of rural Massachusetts, a setting Lovecraft knew intimately. But instead of a quaint pastoral scene, we're given a vision of contamination and decay. The very soil turns grey and dead. The trees twist into grotesque shapes. The fruit grows large and vibrant but tastes foul. This isn't supernatural horror in the traditional sense—it's ecological horror, long before that term existed.

In many ways, The Colour Out of Space is a forerunner of the genre we now call "eco-horror." The meteorite, with its alien essence, doesn't just kill—it corrupts. It seeps into the groundwater, poisons the earth, and alters the DNA of every living thing it touches. The Gardner family, who live on the doomed farm, don't die from violence or malice. They wither, mentally and physically, becoming barely recognizable as human by the end. Their suffering is slow, intimate, and incurable. There is no ritual that can banish the "colour," no hero who can save the day. The horror is impersonal. It arrives, it consumes, and it leaves—leaving madness in its wake.

This theme of scientific unknowability is central to the story. The meteorite is examined by experts, but it defies all explanation. It shrinks over time, its material composition is unstable, and its properties are inconsistent with anything known to science. One of the spheres of influence Lovecraft was deeply concerned with was the rise of materialist science in the early twentieth century—the growing realization that the more we understood about the universe, the more alien and inhospitable it appeared.

In The Colour Out of Space, science is powerless. The best minds can't explain the phenomenon, and the everyday people who live with it go mad trying to survive it. This bleak outlook is not simply cynicism—it's a rejection of the human-centered worldview that dominated Western thought for centuries. Lovecraft insists that we are not the masters of our world. We are fragile, ignorant, and vulnerable. The forces that surround us—cosmic, natural, or otherwise—do not need to hate us to destroy us. Indifference is enough.

At the same time, the story is deeply human in its tragedy. The Gardners are not bad people. They are decent, hardworking, rural Americans who find themselves at the mercy of something they cannot understand. Their suffering is wrenching because it is undeserved and unstoppable. The father, Nahum Gardner, tries to hold his family together but is ultimately broken by the ordeal. His wife and children either go insane or waste away. Their farm becomes a site of unmarked devastation—a place so horrifying that even decades later, nothing will grow there.

The "blasted heath" becomes a metaphor for the limits of human control over nature and knowledge. It is a cursed place, not through magic or divine punishment, but through exposure to something utterly alien. The more one contemplates the implications of this story, the more disturbing it becomes. Its horror is cumulative, not because of any specific monster or jump scare, but because it implies that we are surrounded by potential unknowns—quiet, colorless invaders that could strike at any moment, without purpose or warning.

Why The Colour Out of Space Still Matters

More than any other story by Lovecraft, The Colour Out of Space distills the essence of his worldview into a single, concentrated narrative. It embodies the terror of the unknown and the unknowable, and it dramatizes the collapse of the human psyche in the face of cosmic indifference. This story has influenced an entire century of horror writers, filmmakers, and thinkers. From Stephen King's The Tommyknockers to Alex Garland's Annihilation, the echoes of The Colour Out of Space can be felt in any tale where science meets mystery and loses.

In many ways, the story predicted our current anxieties. Climate change, nuclear contamination, and the unintended consequences of scientific advancement have become very real, very urgent fears. The idea that a substance could seep into the land and alter everything—without malice, without logic—is no longer science fiction. Lovecraft didn't write this as an environmental parable, but his vision of creeping, invisible ruin feels more prophetic than ever.

Moreover, the story is a masterclass in restraint. Lovecraft doesn't give us a detailed description of the "colour." He doesn't show us the transformations directly. Instead, we hear about them from a secondary narrator recounting the impressions of others. This method makes the horror more powerful. By refusing to show the full shape of the threat, Lovecraft lets our imaginations do the work—and our imaginations, guided by his suggestion of the incomprehensible, often invent something more terrifying than any visual could.

This modern adaptation aims to preserve that power while making the story more accessible to contemporary readers. Lovecraft's original prose is dense, archaic, and sometimes awkward by today's standards. His use of regional dialect, long sentences, and antiquated vocabulary can obscure the story's momentum and tension. This version presents a sentence-by-sentence modernization that retains the narrative voice, atmosphere, and terror of the original but renders it in clear, contemporary English. It is not a simplification—it is an unclouding.

The goal is to ensure that the horror reaches you just as sharply as it did to Lovecraft's first readers. You'll meet Ammi Pierce, a witness marked by grief and trauma, and hear of the Gardners' slow descent into madness. You'll feel the dread rise as the trees sway with unnatural motion, as the water begins to shimmer strangely, as the crops glow with unnatural ripeness. And you will not forget the final revelation—the true, final horror of what still lingers in the soil beneath the modern reservoir.

The Colour Out of Space is not just a story. It is a philosophical challenge, a warning, and a vision. It asks you to stare into the abyss—not to find evil, but to discover indifference. In doing so, it reveals how fragile our understanding of reality truly is. As you read this adaptation, prepare not for a monster, but for a force. Not for answers, but for awe. You are entering a story that is as much about perception as it is about destruction. And when you leave, the world may seem just a little less safe, and a little less knowable.

Welcome to the colour.

The Colour Out of Space

West of Arkham, the hills grow wild, and deep valleys hide forests untouched by human hands. In the narrow, shadowy hollows, trees bend in strange ways, and small streams flow quietly, never touched by sunlight. On the softer slopes, there used to be old rocky farms. Their short cottages, covered in moss, sat silently beside huge stone outcroppings, keeping the secrets of old New England. But those farms are empty now. The chimneys are falling apart, and the walls are starting to bulge under the weight of sagging roofs.

The families who lived there long ago have left, and newcomers don't stay. French-Canadians, Italians, and Poles have all tried to settle in the area, but they never last. It's not because of anything you can see, hear, or touch. It's something people just feel—something imagined. The place stirs the mind in strange ways and brings bad dreams. That might be why people avoid it. Ammi Pierce, an old man who's not quite right in the head, is the only one who still lives nearby and speaks of what happened long ago. He only dares to talk because his home sits close to the open fields and roads that connect to Arkham.

There used to be a road that cut straight across the hills and valleys, right where the dead land now lies. But people stopped using it and built a new road that bends far to the south. You can still see bits of the old road through the weeds, though soon even those may disappear when parts of the valley are flooded for a new reservoir. Then the trees will be cleared, and the dead land will sink beneath calm, blue water. The surface will shine under the sun, hiding the past beneath it. The strange events of the past will vanish under the water, joining the secrets of the deep sea and the ancient earth.

When I went up into the hills to help plan the reservoir, people warned me the place was bad. They told me this in Arkham, an old town full of ghost stories and tales of witches, so I assumed it was just something grandmothers whispered to scare children. The name "blasted heath" sounded dramatic, and I figured it came from some old legend. But then I saw the twisted valleys and hills myself, and I stopped wondering. The place had a mystery of its own. Even in daylight, the shadows never fully left. The trees were too close together, their trunks too thick to be natural. The spaces between them were silent and dim, and the ground was soft with layers of moss and years of decay.

In the clearer spots along the old road, there were broken-down farms. Some still had buildings, others had just one or two, and a few had only a crumbling chimney or a half-buried cellar. Weeds and thorny plants had taken over. You could hear small animals sneaking through the brush. Everything felt uneasy, like the world wasn't quite right. It was like looking at a painting where something was just off. I didn't blame the newcomers for leaving. It wasn't a place where you could rest. It looked like something out of a dark story or a haunting old picture—something meant to be avoided.

But even with everything else, nothing was as disturbing as the blasted heath. I realized it the moment I saw it, sitting at the bottom of a wide valley. No other name could describe it better, and no other place could match the name. It felt like someone had created that phrase just to describe this exact spot. I thought maybe a fire had caused the damage, but I couldn't understand why, after all these years, nothing had grown back. The five acres of land were bare and gray, like something had eaten a hole through the forest and fields. Most of it lay on the north side of the old road, but it stretched a little to the other side as well. I didn't want to go near it, but my work forced me to pass through.

The land was completely empty—no plants at all— just a fine layer of gray dust or ash that the wind never seemed to move. The trees nearby looked weak and sick, and many had already died, their trunks rotting along the edge of the heath. As I walked quickly past, I saw the broken bricks and stones of what used to be a chimney and cellar, and an old well that sat open like a black mouth in the ground. The foul air rising from it twisted the sunlight in strange ways. Even the dark forest ahead felt more welcoming than this place, and I finally understood why people in Arkham whispered about it with fear. There were no houses or ruins nearby; even long ago, the place must have been isolated and empty. When evening came, I didn't want to go past it again, so I took the long, winding road south to return to town. I found myself hoping for clouds to cover the sky, because something about the open, starry space above made me deeply uneasy.

That night, I asked some older folks in Arkham about the blasted heath and what they meant by "the strange days," a phrase I kept hearing them say with nervous looks. But I didn't get clear answers. I was surprised to learn the events they spoke of weren't old legends—they had happened in their own lifetimes, back in the 1880s. A family had vanished or died, though nobody would give details. Everyone told me not to listen to the wild stories of old Ammi Pierce. So the next morning, I decided to visit him. I had heard he lived alone in a crumbling old house, just where the forest began to grow thick and dark. The place looked incredibly old and gave off a faint, musty smell that clings to houses left standing for too long.

I had to knock several times before Ammi finally came to the door. He moved slowly and seemed nervous, and it was clear he wasn't happy to see me. He wasn't as weak as I expected, but his eyes drooped in a strange way, and his messy clothes and white beard made him look tired and worn-out.

Not sure how to get him talking, I pretended to be there for work. I mentioned my surveying job and asked some general questions about the area. To my surprise, he was smarter and more educated than I'd been led to believe. Before long, he understood as much about the project as anyone I'd met in Arkham. He wasn't like the other country folk I'd met near other reservoir sites. He didn't complain about the land being flooded— probably because his house wasn't within the area marked for the lake. In fact, he seemed relieved that the dark old valleys he had known all his life would finally be covered by water. "It's better that way," he said softly. "Better since the strange days." As he spoke, his voice dropped, he leaned forward, and his finger began to shake as he pointed.

That's when I heard the story. As he rambled on in a hoarse whisper, I felt chills over and over again, even though it was a warm summer day. Sometimes I had to help him stay focused, remind him of things, or make sense of the science he half-remembered from old professors. His thoughts wandered often, and his logic didn't always follow. But when he finally finished, I didn't blame him for losing his mind a little. And I understood why people in Arkham avoided the topic of the blasted heath.

Before sunset, I hurried back to my hotel, not wanting to be out under the stars. The next day, I returned to Boston and quit my job. I couldn't go back into that dark, tangled forest or pass by that gray, dead land again—especially not near that gaping black well beside the broken bricks. The reservoir will be finished soon, and all the old secrets will be buried deep under the water. But even then, I don't think I could ever visit that place again at night—not under those eerie stars. And no one could ever convince me to drink the new water coming to Arkham.

Old Ammi said it all started with a meteorite. Before that, there hadn't been any strange stories in the area— not since the days of the witch trials. Even back then, the nearby woods weren't considered scary. People were more afraid of a small island in the Miskatonic

River, where the devil was said to gather near a mysterious stone altar, older than the Native Americans. These woods weren't haunted, and their strange shadows didn't seem threatening—at least not until the strange days began.

That's when a bright white cloud appeared in the sky at noon, followed by a series of loud explosions, and then a column of smoke rising from deep in the forest. By nightfall, all of Arkham had heard about a huge rock that fell from the sky and buried itself next to the well on Nahum Gardner's land. His house once stood where the blasted heath would eventually be—a neat white house surrounded by healthy gardens and orchards.

Nahum had come into town to talk about the strange rock and stopped by Ammi Pierce's house on the way. Ammi was forty at the time, and the strange events stayed clear in his memory. He and his wife joined three professors from Miskatonic University, who rushed out the next morning to examine the meteorite. They were confused when Nahum said it seemed smaller than the day before. As he showed them the brownish mound near his old well, he mentioned it had shrunk. The professors didn't believe it—rocks don't shrink, they said.

The meteorite was still hot to the touch, and Nahum claimed it had glowed slightly at night. When the professors tested it with a hammer, they found it unusually soft—almost like clay. They had to scoop out a piece rather than chip it off. They put the sample in an old metal pail from Nahum's kitchen because it was still too hot to touch. On the way back, they stopped at Ammi's again, and his wife noted that the rock was getting smaller and burning through the bottom of the pail. It wasn't very big, but maybe they had taken even less than they thought.

The next day, in June of 1882, the professors returned, very excited. As they passed Ammi's place, they told him the sample had done strange things in the lab. It completely vanished after being placed in a glass beaker—and the beaker disappeared too. They guessed the rock had some odd connection to silicon. It didn't behave like any normal material. It didn't react to heat or chemicals, and it gave no signs of gas or vapor when tested. It stayed solid at all temperatures, even under the strongest flames. It was soft enough to bend easily, and it glowed brightly in the dark. The scientists at the college became fascinated by it.

They kept testing it with different chemicals—water, hydrochloric acid, nitric acid, even aqua regia—but nothing worked. The rock just hissed and bubbled, but didn't change. Ammi didn't remember all the details clearly, but when I listed the different substances, some rang a bell—ammonia, caustic soda, alcohol, ether, and several more. The piece of rock kept getting smaller and slowly cooled, but the chemicals didn't seem to affect it at all. Still, it was clearly metal. It was magnetic, and after being soaked in acid, faint patterns appeared on it—like the ones found on iron from space. Once it cooled more, they started keeping the pieces in glass containers. They left all the small fragments in a beaker on a shelf—but by the next morning, both the rock and the glass were gone. All that remained was a burned mark on the wood where the beaker had been.

The professors told Ammi everything as they stopped by his door again, and once more, he joined them to see the strange rock from the stars—though this time, his wife stayed home. The meteorite had definitely shrunk now, and even the serious scientists couldn't deny it. Around the fading brown lump near the well, the earth had collapsed slightly, and the rock that had once been seven feet wide was now less than five. It was still warm, and they carefully studied it as they broke off another, larger chunk with hammer and chisel. This time, they dug deeper into the rock—and found something surprising.

Inside, they uncovered what looked like a large, colored bubble hidden within the stone. The color was strange and hard to describe, similar to the strange colors they'd seen when testing its light spectrum. It was shiny, and when they tapped it, it seemed hollow and fragile. One professor gave it a firm hit with the hammer. It popped with a soft crack—and vanished instantly. Nothing came out of it. The only thing left was an empty, round space about three inches wide. The scientists guessed there were more of these hidden bubbles inside, waiting to be found as the rock continued to disappear.

Guesses didn't help, so after a failed attempt to drill for more of the strange bubbles, the scientists left with their latest sample. But in the lab, it was just as confusing as the first one. It was soft like clay, gave off heat and a faint glow, reacted oddly with strong acids, disappeared in air, and somehow destroyed itself when it touched anything made of silicon. It had an unknown color pattern, but other than that, no one could figure out what it really was. In the end, the college experts had to admit they had no idea what they were dealing with. It wasn't from Earth. It came from somewhere far beyond, and it followed rules that didn't match anything we know.

That night, a thunderstorm rolled in. The next day, when the scientists went back to Nahum's farm, they were disappointed. The rock must've had some weird electrical property, because it kept getting struck by lightning. Nahum said it was hit six times in one hour. After the storm passed, the only thing left was a torn-up hole near the old well, half-filled with dirt from the collapse. Digging didn't help, and the scientists confirmed the rock was completely gone. They had failed, and all they could do was go back to test the small piece they had stored safely in a lead case. That last fragment lasted about a week, but they still didn't learn anything useful. When it disappeared, it left no trace behind. In time, the scientists even began to doubt what they had seen, wondering if that strange sample from some other world had really existed at all.

Naturally, the newspapers in Arkham wrote a lot about the meteorite, especially since college professors were involved. Reporters came to interview Nahum and his family. Even a Boston paper sent a writer. Nahum quickly became something of a local celebrity. He was a thin, friendly man of about fifty, living with his wife and three sons on a peaceful farm in the valley. He and Ammi often visited each other, along with their wives, and Ammi always spoke highly of him. Nahum seemed a little proud of the attention his farm had received and talked a lot about the meteorite in the following weeks.

That July and August were especially hot, and Nahum spent long days harvesting hay from the ten-acre field across Chapman's Brook. His wagon carved deep tracks through the shaded paths. The work wore him out more than usual, and he started to feel the weight of age creeping up on him.

Then came the time for harvesting fruit. The apples and pears began to ripen, and Nahum was thrilled. He said his orchard had never looked better. The fruit was unusually large, shiny, and so plentiful that he ordered extra barrels to handle the big harvest. But when the fruit finally ripened, it brought disappointment. Despite how beautiful it looked, none of it was safe to eat. The apples and pears had a strange bitter and sick taste. Even a small bite made people feel sick. The same was true for the melons and tomatoes. Nahum sadly realized his entire harvest was ruined. Thinking quickly, he blamed the meteorite for poisoning the ground, and he was thankful that most of his other crops were planted in the higher fields along the road.

Winter came early and was especially harsh. Ammi didn't see Nahum as often and noticed that he looked more troubled than usual. The rest of the family also seemed quieter, staying away from church and social gatherings in the area. No one could figure out why, though the family sometimes mentioned feeling sick or unsettled. Nahum gave the clearest explanation when he said he had seen strange tracks in the snow. They looked like they came from squirrels, rabbits, or foxes— but something about them seemed wrong. He wasn't clear about what was off, just that they didn't look or behave like normal animal tracks should.

At first, Ammi didn't pay much attention to Nahum's story. But one night, while riding his sleigh past the Gardner house under the moonlight, a rabbit ran across the road. Its jumps were far too long. Even Ammi's horse was startled and almost bolted. After that, Ammi began to take Nahum's stories more seriously. He also started wondering why the Gardner family's dogs looked scared and shaky every morning. Eventually, it came out that the dogs had almost stopped barking altogether.

In February, the McGregor boys from nearby Meadow Hill were out hunting woodchucks. Near the Gardner farm, they shot a strange one. Its body was oddly shaped in ways they couldn't explain, and its face had a look no one had ever seen on a woodchuck before. The boys were so disturbed they threw it away immediately, so all that remained were their weird stories. By then, horses had begun to shy away when passing the Gardner property. Whispers and rumors were spreading fast, and the start of a new local legend was already taking shape.

People started saying that snow melted faster near Nahum Gardner's farm than anywhere else. In early March, folks gathered at Potter's general store in Clark's Corners to talk about something strange. That morning, Stephen Rice had passed Nahum's place and noticed skunk cabbages sprouting near the muddy woods across the road. They were huge—bigger than anyone had ever seen—and their colors were weird, almost impossible to describe. Their shapes looked unnatural, and Stephen's horse got spooked by a strange smell that he couldn't compare to anything he'd ever known.

That afternoon, more people drove by to see the bizarre plants, and everyone agreed that they weren't normal. They reminded folks of the bad fruit from the previous fall, and word spread fast that the ground on Nahum's farm was poisoned. Everyone blamed the meteorite, and since the scientists had said the stone was strange, a few farmers reached out to them for answers.

The scientists came to visit Nahum but didn't believe much of what they heard. They weren't interested in local superstitions and didn't want to jump to conclusions. They admitted the plants were strange, but said skunk cabbages were always a little odd. Maybe the meteor had left some unusual mineral in the soil, but they figured it would wash away soon enough. As for the odd animal tracks and the scared horses, they chalked it up to local gossip. In their view, country people often made up stories, and they didn't think there was anything serious going on. After that, the professors kept their distance. Only one of them remembered the event later, over a year and a half afterward, when he analyzed two samples of dust during a police investigation. He noticed that the color of the skunk cabbage looked a lot like one of the unusual light bands from the meteorite and the strange bubble inside it. At first, the dust samples showed the same colors, but eventually, they faded.

Around Nahum's house, the trees started to bud too early, and at night, they moved oddly in the wind. Nahum's second son, Thaddeus, who was fifteen, said the trees swayed even when there was no wind, though no one believed him at the time. Still, people couldn't deny something felt off. The whole Gardner family started acting strangely—they would stop and listen quietly, though they didn't seem to be listening for anything specific. It happened most when they seemed half-asleep, and these strange moments happened more and more often. Before long, everyone was saying there was something wrong with Nahum's family.

When the early spring flowers bloomed, they also had a strange color—not quite like the skunk cabbages, but still not natural. Nahum brought a few to Arkham and showed them to the local newspaper editor, who only wrote a joking article that made fun of the villagers' fears. Nahum shouldn't have told him about the butterflies, either. The big mourning-cloak butterflies had started acting strangely around the flowers, which only made the whole thing seem more unsettling.

In April, things got worse. People started avoiding the road near Nahum's house, and soon, hardly anyone used it at all. The plants became even stranger. The orchard trees blossomed in odd colors, and unusual plants grew through the rocky soil around the house and in the pasture nearby. Only a trained botanist could've recognized them as anything close to the region's native plants. The normal greens of grass and leaves were still there, but everything else took on sickly, shifting shades—bright, chaotic colors that didn't belong in nature. Some flowers, like the "Dutchman's breeches," looked twisted and threatening, and even the bloodroots appeared unnaturally bold in color. Ammi and the Gardners noticed that many of the strange colors looked like the bubble inside the meteor.

Nahum plowed and planted his ten-acre field and the higher lot near the road but left the land around his house untouched. He knew it was hopeless and hoped the summer plants might soak up the poison from the soil. By now, he was used to the feeling that something invisible was always nearby. The way his neighbors avoided him made him feel worse, but it was his wife who suffered the most. The boys were better off because they went to school every day, but even they couldn't ignore the whispers. Thaddeus, being sensitive, was especially shaken by it all.

In May, the insects arrived, and Nahum's farm turned into a buzzing, crawling nightmare. Many of the bugs looked off, and their movements didn't match anything the family had ever seen. They were also active at night in ways that didn't make sense. The Gardners began staying up to watch, staring into the dark without knowing exactly what they were looking for. Eventually, everyone in the family admitted Thaddeus had been right—the trees really did move without wind. Mrs. Gardner saw it one night from her window. A maple tree's thick branches swayed under the moonlight, even though the air was still. She told herself it must be the sap, but deep down, she knew something was wrong with everything growing around them.

But the next strange discovery didn't come from the Gardners at all. They'd grown too used to the weirdness. Instead, it came from a nervous windmill salesman from Bolton who didn't know the local rumors. One night, while passing the Gardner farm in his buggy, he saw something strange. He later shared his story in Arkham, and it ended up as a short note in the newspaper. That's how most of the farmers—Nahum included—heard about it. The night had been dark, and the salesman's lights were dim, but around the farm in the valley, he said the darkness didn't seem as thick. All the plants— grass, trees, flowers—gave off a soft glow. At one point, a small patch of that glowing light seemed to move on its own near the barn.

At first, the grass near the Gardner house looked fine, and the cows still grazed in the nearby field. But toward the end of May, the milk started to go bad. Nahum moved the cows up to higher ground, and the milk improved. Soon after, the grass and leaves began changing—turning gray and strangely brittle, like they could crumble if touched.

By then, Ammi was the only person still visiting, and even he came less and less. When school let out, the Gardner family became completely isolated. Sometimes they had Ammi run errands in town for them. Everyone could see they were getting weaker, both in body and mind. So when word spread that Mrs. Gardner had gone mad, no one was really surprised.

It happened in June, around the same time the meteorite had fallen the year before. She began screaming about things in the air she couldn't describe. Her words didn't make much sense—mostly just verbs and pronouns. She said things moved and changed and fluttered. Her ears picked up feelings more than sounds. She said something was draining her, that something was clinging to her and needed to be stopped. She claimed the walls and windows shifted during the night and nothing was ever still.

Nahum didn't send her away. As long as she wasn't a danger to herself or others, he let her wander the house. Even when her expression became disturbing, he didn't act. But when the boys started to fear her—especially Thaddeus, who nearly fainted from the faces she made—Nahum finally locked her in the attic. By July, she had stopped talking and crawled on all fours. Later that month, Nahum started to believe she glowed faintly in the dark, just like the plants around the house.

Not long before that, the horses had panicked one night. Something scared them so badly that they thrashed in their stalls, kicking and neighing in terror. Nahum opened the stable, and they bolted like wild deer.

It took a week to find them all, but by then, they were too far gone—wild, broken, and impossible to control. They had to be put down.

Nahum borrowed a horse from Ammi to help with haying, but it refused to go near the barn. It whinnied and refused to move forward. In the end, Nahum had to leave it in the yard while the workers dragged the heavy wagon close to the hayloft by hand.

Meanwhile, the plants continued to change. Everything was turning gray and brittle. The once-bright flowers lost their strange colors and faded into gray. The fruit was stunted, tasteless, and lifeless. The asters, goldenrod, roses, zinnias, and hollyhocks looked so twisted and awful that Nahum's oldest son, Zenas, cut them all down. Around that time, the swollen bugs started to die off—even the bees that had left their hives and flown to the woods.

By September, most of the plants had crumbled into gray powder. Nahum feared the trees would die before the poison in the soil could be cleansed. His wife began having awful screaming fits, and the whole family was constantly on edge. They avoided people, and when school started again, the boys didn't go back.

During one of Ammi's rare visits, he was the first to notice the well water had changed. It tasted bad—not quite rotten, not quite salty, but definitely wrong. He warned Nahum to dig a new well farther uphill, at least until things got better. But Nahum ignored him. By that time, he was numb to the strange and horrible things happening around him. He and the boys kept drinking the water, eating poorly cooked meals, and doing their chores like lifeless machines. They looked like people already halfway gone—just waiting for something terrible they couldn't avoid.

In September, Thaddeus lost his mind after a trip to the well. He had gone with a pail and came back screaming, waving his arms, sometimes giggling, sometimes whispering about "the moving colors down there." Having two family members go mad was horrible, but Nahum stayed strong. He let Thaddeus roam freely for a while, but when the boy started to fall and hurt himself, Nahum locked him in the attic across from his mother. The two of them would scream at each other from behind locked doors, and it was terrifying—especially for little Merwin, who began imagining they were speaking in some awful, otherworldly language.

Merwin became more restless after Thaddeus was locked away. He had been Merwin's closest friend and playmate.

Around the same time, the animals began dying. The chickens turned gray and died quickly, and when they were cut open, their meat was dry and rotten. The pigs grew unnaturally fat before suffering horrible changes no one could explain. Their meat was no good. Nahum was at a loss. No local vet would come near the farm, and even the vet from Arkham had no idea what was happening. The pigs became brittle and broke apart before dying. Their eyes and snouts changed in disturbing ways. What made it worse was that they hadn't eaten any of the poisoned plants.

Then the cows got sick too. Sometimes just one part of their body would shrivel up unnaturally, other times their whole body was affected. They always ended up dying, turning gray and brittle like the pigs. No one could figure out how it was happening. The animals were kept in locked barns—nothing had bitten them, nothing had broken in. It had to be a disease, but no one had ever seen anything like it.

By harvest time, no animals were left alive on the farm. The livestock and chickens were all dead. The dogs had run away, all three of them disappearing in one night and never coming back. The five cats had vanished earlier, though no one noticed much since there weren't any mice left, and only Mrs. Gardner had cared for them.

On October 19th, Nahum stumbled into Ammi's house with terrible news. Thaddeus had died in his attic room—and the way it happened was too awful to describe. Nahum had buried what was left of him in the family graveyard behind the house. The door had stayed locked, and the small window was still barred, so nothing could've gotten in from outside. But what he found reminded him of what had happened in the barn.

Ammi and his wife did their best to comfort Nahum, but even being near him filled the room with dread. It felt like something awful clung to the Gardners, like just being around them brought a sense of fear that couldn't be explained. Ammi went back with Nahum to the farm, even though he really didn't want to. He tried to calm little Merwin, who was sobbing uncontrollably. Zenas didn't react to anything anymore—he just stared blankly and did whatever his father told him. Ammi actually felt that this numbness might be a small mercy.

Sometimes they heard faint screams from the attic, and when Ammi gave Nahum a questioning look, he said his wife was growing weaker. As night fell, Ammi found a way to leave. Even their friendship wasn't enough to keep him there when the plants outside started glowing faintly and the trees seemed to sway without any wind. Luckily, Ammi wasn't very imaginative—otherwise, his mind might've broken under the weight of everything he'd seen. As it was, his thoughts were already beginning to fray. He rushed home as the disturbing sounds of the madwoman and the terrified child echoed in his ears.

Three days later, Nahum burst into Ammi's kitchen early in the morning. Ammi wasn't home, so Nahum told his story to Mrs. Pierce, who listened in growing fear. This time, it was Merwin—he had vanished. The boy had gone out at night with a lantern and a pail to get water, and he never came back. For days, he'd been falling apart, barely aware of what he was doing, jumping at everything. There had been a loud scream from the yard, but by the time Nahum reached the door, Merwin was gone. The lantern's glow had vanished, and there was no sign of the boy.

At first, Nahum thought both the lantern and pail were missing too. But after a long night searching the woods and fields, he found something strange near the well. There was a misshapen, partly melted lump of iron that had once been the lantern. A twisted pail and some warped metal bands lay nearby, half-melted. That was all that was left. Nahum couldn't even imagine what had happened. Mrs. Pierce was speechless, and when Ammi got home and heard the story, he couldn't guess either.

Merwin was gone. There was no point telling the neighbors—they already avoided the Gardners. Telling the people in Arkham wouldn't help either; they laughed off everything. First Thaddeus, now Merwin. Nahum felt like something was crawling closer, waiting to show itself. He knew his time was almost up and asked Ammi to look after his wife and Zenas if they lived longer than him. He believed it was some kind of punishment, though he didn't know what for—he had always tried to live a good and honest life.

For over two weeks, Ammi didn't see or hear from Nahum. Finally, worried about what might've happened, he pushed past his fear and went to the farm. There was no smoke coming from the chimney, and for a moment, Ammi feared the worst. The farm looked lifeless—gray, brittle grass and leaves covered the ground. Vines were falling apart on the walls and rooftops, and the bare trees looked like they were reaching up toward the gloomy November sky in a way that felt angry or twisted. Ammi couldn't shake the feeling that even the trees had changed somehow.

But Nahum was still alive. He was weak and lying on a couch in the cold kitchen, but he was awake and able to give simple commands to Zenas. The room was freezing, and Ammi started to shiver. Nahum, seeing this, rasped at Zenas to bring more wood. The big fireplace was empty, and cold wind blew soot down the chimney. As Zenas fetched more wood, Nahum asked Ammi if he felt warmer now.

That's when Ammi understood—Nahum's mind had finally broken. The man had gone through so much grief that his mind had shut down completely. Nothing could hurt him anymore.

Ammi tried to ask gentle questions, but he couldn't get any clear answers about what had happened to Zenas. "In the well—he lives in the well," was all Nahum would say, his mind clearly clouded. That made Ammi think of Nahum's wife, and he quickly changed the subject.

"Nabby? Why, here she is!" Nahum said with surprise, waving toward the house. Realizing he'd have to check for himself, Ammi left the dazed man on the couch, took the keys hanging by the door, and went upstairs. The air in the attic was hot and foul, and everything was silent. Four doors lined the hallway, but only one was locked. Ammi tried several keys, and the third one finally worked. With shaking hands, he opened the low white door.

The room was very dark. The window was tiny and partly covered by rough wooden bars, so it was hard to see anything. The smell was overwhelming. Ammi had to back out and catch his breath in another room before he could go in. When he returned, he noticed a dark shape in the corner. As he looked closer, he let out a scream. While screaming, he thought something briefly blocked the light from the window. A second later, he felt something brush past him—like a wave of foul air. Strange colors danced before his eyes, and though terror numbed his mind, part of him remembered the weird glowing bubble inside the meteor and the unnatural plants that had grown in the spring.

What stood in the corner was something so horrific, Ammi could only compare it to what had happened to Thaddeus and the animals. But the worst part was that it moved—slowly and visibly—as it crumbled.

Ammi never gave me many details about what he saw in that room. The thing in the corner never appeared again in his story as something that moved. Some horrors are better left unspoken, and sometimes even merciful actions can be judged harshly. From what I understood, there was nothing left in that attic that could move anymore. Whatever was still capable of motion couldn't be allowed to stay alive. Most people would've fainted or lost their minds. But Ammi, even shaken, stayed in control. He stepped out of the attic and locked the door behind him. Now he had to deal with Nahum—he needed food, care, and to be moved somewhere safe.

As Ammi started down the stairs, he heard a loud thud below. He thought he also heard a scream that was suddenly cut off. The memory of that strange, sticky air brushing against him in the attic came rushing back. Had his shout or his presence awakened something? Frozen with fear, he listened harder. There were more sounds now—something heavy dragging across the floor, mixed with a squelching noise, like something wet and unnatural. His mind, already on edge, made a connection with what he had just seen upstairs. What nightmare had he stumbled into?

Ammi didn't know whether to move forward or run. He stood frozen on the narrow, boxed-in staircase, his heart racing. Every detail burned itself into his mind— the sounds, the darkness, the steep stairs, the thick silence. And then, to his horror, he realized that all the wood—stairs, walls, beams—was glowing faintly in the dark.

Suddenly, his horse outside let out a terrified whinny, followed by the sound of it bolting away in a panic. The buggy clattered wildly, then faded into the distance. Ammi was alone now. Something else had happened, too—a splash, like something hitting water. The well.

He'd left his horse untied near it, and maybe a wheel had knocked a stone into the water. Meanwhile, that pale glow still clung to the ancient wood. How old was this house? Most of it had been built before 1700.

Then he heard a soft scratching sound from downstairs. He gripped the heavy stick he'd grabbed in the attic and forced himself to keep going. He stepped into the kitchen—but stopped dead in his tracks. What he was looking for wasn't in the same spot anymore. It had come toward him. It was still alive, in a way, though clearly dying. Ammi didn't know if it had crawled on its own or had been pulled by something unseen. But whatever had happened, death had already started its work. The body was breaking down fast—turning gray, cracking, and falling apart.

Ammi couldn't bring himself to touch it. He just stared in horror at the ruined thing that had once been a man. He leaned close and whispered, "What was it, Nahum—what was it?"

The twisted, cracked lips barely moved, but they forced out one final answer.

"Nothing... there's nothing left... that color—it hurts... it feels cold and wet, but it still burns... it's alive, hiding down in the well... I saw it... it looked like smoke... kind of like spring flowers... the well glowed at night...

Thad, Merwin, Zenas... everything that was alive... it took all their life away... I think it came with the stone... whatever it is, it spreads poison... I don't even know what it wants...

That round thing those college guys dug out of the rock... they smashed it... it had the same color... just like the plants and flowers... maybe there were more of them... like seeds... and they grew... I saw one for the first time this week... I think it fed on Zenas... he used to be so full of life...

It messes up your mind before it takes over... burns you from the inside out... it's in the water... you were right, Ammi... the water's bad... Zenas went to the well and never came back... you can't run from it... it pulls you in... you know it's coming, but you still can't stop it...

I kept seeing it after Zenas disappeared... again and again... where's Nabby, Ammi? My head's not working right... I don't remember the last time I fed her... if we don't watch out, it'll get her too...

It's just a color... but sometimes when the sun goes down, her face has that same color... and it burns, and it takes... it came from somewhere far from here... not like our world... one of the professors said that... and he was right...

Be careful, Ammi... it's not over yet... it won't stop until it takes everything…"

That was the last thing Nahum said. He couldn't speak anymore—his body gave out completely. Ammi gently covered what was left of him with a red-checked tablecloth, then stumbled out the back door and into the open fields. He climbed up to the ten-acre pasture and walked home the long way, taking the road through the woods. He didn't dare pass by the well, the one his horses had run from. He had seen it through the window before he left, and noticed that no stones were missing from the rim. So the splash he heard earlier hadn't been from the buggy hitting it. Something else had gone into that well… something that finished off Nahum.

By the time Ammi made it back to his house, his horse and buggy had arrived ahead of him, throwing his wife into a panic. He calmed her without giving any real explanation, then immediately headed to Arkham to report what had happened. He told the authorities that the Gardner family was gone. He didn't give details— just said Nahum and Nabby were dead, that Thaddeus had already been known to be gone, and that the deaths seemed to be from the same strange illness that had killed their animals. He also said Merwin and Zenas had disappeared.

The police had a lot of questions, and in the end, Ammi had to return to the farm with them. They brought along three officers, the county coroner, a medical examiner, and the vet who had seen the sick livestock. Ammi didn't want to go back, especially so late in the day, but it helped to have others with him.

They all traveled in a wagon behind Ammi's buggy and reached the Gardner farm around 4 p.m. Even the most experienced officers were shaken by what they found. The attic, the kitchen, the whole house—it was all horrifying. The farm's gray, lifeless landscape was bad enough, but the remains under the tablecloth and in the attic were worse than anyone could have imagined. No one could look at them for long. The medical examiner said there was barely anything left to study. Still, he collected samples.

Later, at the college lab, two small bottles of dust were analyzed. Under the spectroscope, both showed unknown colors—bands of light that matched the strange readings from the meteor a year before. But within a month, those colors vanished. What remained in the dust were mostly common minerals like carbonates and alkaline phosphates.

Ammi hadn't planned to tell the group about the well, but when a detective questioned him, he admitted that Nahum had always feared something down there. He never even tried to look for Merwin or Zenas inside it. Once the group heard that, they insisted on checking the well immediately. Ammi was forced to stay while they pulled up bucket after bucket of foul-smelling water, dumping it onto the ground. The smell was so bad near the end that the men had to hold their noses.

Thankfully, the water level was lower than expected, so the job didn't take too long. What they found inside doesn't need to be described in detail. Merwin and Zenas were both there, or at least part of them was. Their remains were mostly bones. There was also a small deer and a large dog in similar condition, along with bones from smaller animals. The sludge at the bottom of the well was oddly soft and bubbling. One man climbed down using handholds and pushed a long pole into the mud. It sank easily, without hitting any solid ground.

By then, twilight had set in, so lanterns were brought from the house. When it was clear they wouldn't find anything else, everyone went inside. They gathered in the old sitting room while the dim light of the half-moon cast a pale glow over the lifeless farm outside.

No one could figure out what had truly happened. The case left the men confused and disturbed. Nothing they saw seemed to fit together. The dying plants, the strange sickness in both animals and people, the way Merwin and Zenas had vanished into the well—it didn't add up. The locals had their theories, but the officials refused to believe anything unnatural had occurred. Maybe the meteor had poisoned the ground, but how did that explain the sickness of people and animals who hadn't eaten anything grown there? Could it have been the well water? Possibly. It would need to be tested. But what kind of madness could drive two boys to jump into that cursed well?

And why had everything become so dry, brittle, and gray?

The coroner, sitting by a window that looked out over the yard, was the first to notice the strange light coming from the well. Night had fully arrived, and the ground already looked faintly lit—not just from the moonlight, but from something else. This glow was real and steady, shooting up from the darkness like a weak beam from a searchlight. The light reflected off small puddles of water nearby. Its color was strange, and when the other men gathered by the window, Ammi suddenly jerked back. He recognized that awful color. He had seen it before—and he was afraid of what it meant.

He had spotted that color in a strange, brittle bubble inside the meteor rock that had fallen two summers ago. He'd seen it again in the twisted plants that grew in spring. He even thought he'd seen a flash of it that morning, on the small barred window of the attic where horrible things had happened. That time, a foul-smelling mist had brushed past him—and then Nahum had been taken by something that matched that same strange light. Nahum had said so before he died. He said it looked like the bubble and the plants. After that, someone ran into the yard, something splashed in the well, and now that same well was glowing with that awful, sickly color again.

Even in that terrifying moment, Ammi's mind stayed sharp. He couldn't help but wonder—how could he have seen the same kind of mist during the day, against the bright sky, and now again at night as a glowing fog against the ruined land? It didn't make sense. It wasn't natural. He remembered Nahum's final words: "It came from a place where things aren't like they are here... one of the professors said that..."

Outside, the three horses tied to two dried-up trees were panicking. They neighed and stomped the ground. The wagon driver started for the door, maybe to calm them, but Ammi stopped him with a shaky hand on his shoulder. "Don't go out there," he whispered. "There's more going on than we understand. Nahum said something lived in the well—something that steals your life. He said it must've grown from a round thing, like the one we saw in that meteor stone that landed last June. He said it burns and sucks the life out of you. It's like a cloud of color, just like that light out there now. You can barely see it, and you can't explain what it is. Nahum thought it fed on everything that's alive, and got stronger as it did. He saw it just last week. It must've come from far away in space, like those college men said the meteor did. The way it moves and acts—it's nothing like anything on Earth. It came from somewhere else."

So the men waited, unsure of what to do, while the light from the well kept growing stronger. The horses were more frantic than ever, and the yard was full of tension. The old house behind them was filled with fear, pieces of bodies had been found both inside and near the well, and now this strange light was pouring from deep underground. Ammi had stopped the driver without thinking, forgetting that he hadn't been hurt when that strange mist had brushed past him in the attic. But maybe it was for the best. No one will ever really know what was out there that night. So far, the strange thing hadn't harmed anyone with a strong mind, but no one could guess what might've happened in that final moment—especially with the light growing stronger and acting like it had a purpose.

Suddenly, one of the detectives near the window gasped. The others looked at him, then followed his eyes upward. No one needed to speak—they all saw it. Until now, it had only been local gossip, but now it was real. Everyone later whispered the same thing, and that's why no one in Arkham ever talks about those strange days.

It's important to say that there was no wind that evening. One came later, but at that exact moment, everything was still. Even the dry, gray plants and the fringe of the wagon roof didn't move. But high above, the bare tree branches began to twitch. They moved like they were in pain, shaking and jerking wildly, as if something invisible below the ground was pulling on them—something twisted and alive beneath the roots.

No one spoke or even breathed for several seconds. Then, a thick cloud passed over the moon, and the outline of the trees disappeared for a moment. That's when everyone cried out—quiet but scared, their voices almost the same. The fear hadn't gone away with the shadows. In the sudden darkness, they saw hundreds of tiny, creepy lights moving at the tops of the trees. Each little branch glowed like it was on fire, like the ghostly lights seen during storms at sea or the flames in old stories about miracles. It was a horrible sight, like a swarm of glowing bugs that had fed on dead bodies, dancing above a cursed swamp. And the color—it was that same unearthly color Ammi had learned to fear.

The light coming from the well kept getting brighter, filling the air with a feeling of dread so heavy the men couldn't even think clearly. It wasn't just shining anymore—it was flooding out. And as that strange, shapeless color flowed from the well, it rose straight into the sky.

...and in that terrifying moment of deeper darkness, the people watching saw hundreds of tiny, eerie lights wriggling at the tops of the trees. Each branch looked like it was glowing, lit up with a pale, ghostly shine— like strange lightning dancing on the tips.

At the same time, the glowing light from the well kept growing stronger and stronger, filling the group with a heavy feeling of dread and wrongness.

It wasn't just glowing anymore—it was flooding out. The strange, colorless light was rising from the well in a steady stream, as if it were flowing straight up into the sky.

The veterinarian shivered and walked to the front door to slide the heavy extra lock into place. Ammi was shaking too, and since he couldn't find his voice, he had to point and tug at someone's arm to draw attention to the trees, which were glowing more and more. The horses outside were making awful noises, stomping and crying out, but no one inside the old house dared to go out—not even for a huge reward.

The glowing light from the trees kept growing, and their branches seemed to stretch higher and higher, reaching straight up. Even the wooden part of the well was starting to glow. One of the policemen quietly pointed to some sheds and beehives near a stone wall—they were beginning to glow too. The visitors' wagons, though, didn't seem affected yet.

Then there was a loud noise from the road—hooves clapping wildly—and when Ammi turned off the lamp for a clearer view, they realized the panicked gray horses had broken free and run off with the wagon.

That shock broke the silence, and a few of the men began to whisper. "It spreads to everything living that's been near here," the medical examiner muttered. Nobody answered, but the man who'd gone down into the well said his long pole must've disturbed something invisible. "It was horrible," he said. "There was no bottom. Just slime, bubbles, and the feeling that something was down there."

Ammi's own horse outside was still screaming so loudly it almost drowned out his weak, shaking voice as he spoke: "It came from that stone. It grew down there. It took everything alive. It fed on their minds and their bodies—Thad, Merwin, Zenas, Nabby... Nahum was the last. They all drank the water. It got stronger from them. It came from far away, where things aren't like they are here. And now it's going back."

Right then, the strange column of color suddenly flared brighter and started twisting into strange shapes—each person later described it differently. That's when Hero, the tied-up horse, let out a sound no one had ever heard before—not before or since. Everyone in the low-ceilinged sitting room covered their ears, and Ammi turned away from the window, feeling sick and horrified. Words couldn't describe it. When he looked back, Hero was lying still on the moonlit ground, his body crumpled between the broken pieces of the wagon. That was the last they saw of Hero—he was buried the next day.

But there was no time to grieve. A detective silently pointed to something awful happening inside the room. Without the lamp, it was easy to see that a faint glow had started to spread across the room. It lit up the wooden floor where the rug didn't cover it and shimmered along the edges of the windows. The glow crept up the walls, along the shelves, across the mantel, and even onto the doors and furniture. Every minute it grew stronger, and it became clear that anything still alive had to leave the house now.

Ammi led them to the back door and pointed out a path through the fields that led up to the ten-acre pasture. They moved like sleepwalkers, afraid to look back until they were high up on safer ground. They were thankful for the path—there was no way they could have gone past the well. Even walking by the glowing barn and sheds was terrifying, not to mention the shining trees in the orchard, twisted in creepy, unnatural shapes. At least the worst of the movement stayed high in the branches. As they crossed a small bridge over Chapman's Brook, the moon vanished behind thick, black clouds, and they had to feel their way through the darkness until they reached the open meadow.

When they finally turned to look back toward the valley and the Gardner farm, the sight was horrifying. The entire farm was glowing with that strange, unnatural light—buildings, trees, even patches of grass that hadn't yet turned dry and gray. The tree branches were all reaching toward the sky, their tips flickering with weird, toxic-looking flames. The same creepy glow was crawling up the rooftops of the house, barn, and sheds. It looked like something from a nightmare painting, and at the center of it all was that glowing, shifting cloud—the color that didn't belong in this world—bubbling and pulsing with an energy that felt evil and wrong.

Then, all of a sudden, the horrible thing shot straight up into the sky like a rocket or a shooting star. It left no trail behind, just disappeared through a strange round hole in the clouds before anyone could react. No one who saw it would ever forget that moment. Ammi stared blankly at the stars, his eyes locking on Deneb, the bright star in the Cygnus constellation, where the strange color had vanished into the Milky Way.

But just as quickly, his attention snapped back to the valley. He heard crackling. Not a blast—just a loud tearing and breaking, like wood snapping apart. Others would later insist it had been an explosion, but Ammi knew better. And still, the result was just as terrifying. In one wild moment, a burst of sparks and strange material exploded up from the farm, full of colors and shapes that didn't belong in our world. The few people who caught a glimpse of it couldn't even make sense of what they saw. The strange, glowing pieces rose into the sky, following the thing that had already vanished.

Seconds later, those glowing pieces disappeared too. Behind them, the valley was swallowed in total darkness.

No one dared to go back. Around them, the wind picked up, sweeping through the fields and trees like a storm from deep space. It howled and screamed, twisting the landscape in a wild, unnatural frenzy. The group soon realized there was no point in waiting for the moon to shine again on Nahum's place. Whatever had happened there—it was over. And none of them would ever be the same.

Too shaken to speak or guess what had really happened, the seven frightened men walked slowly back toward Arkham along the north road. Ammi was in worse shape than the others. He begged them to walk him all the way to his kitchen instead of continuing to town. He didn't want to go through the twisted, wind-blown woods alone to reach his house by the main road.

Ammi had seen something the others hadn't—something that left him deeply disturbed, though he wouldn't speak of it for many years. While the others had turned away from the valley, Ammi had looked back one last time at the ruined land that had once been home to his unlucky friend. And there, in the shadows, he saw something weakly rise from the same place where that horrible, shapeless thing had flown into the sky. Then it sank back down into the well. It was just a color—but not one found on Earth or in the sky. Ammi recognized it right away. He knew part of that thing was still hiding down there, and that knowledge left him changed forever.

Ammi never went near the place again. It's been forty-four years since that night, but he's stayed far away. He says he'll be glad when the new reservoir covers it for good. I'll be glad too. I didn't like how the sunlight looked near the edge of that abandoned well—it seemed off, somehow. I hope the water in the reservoir stays deep. Either way, I'll never drink from it. And I don't think I'll ever visit Arkham again.

Three of the men went back the next morning to see what was left. But there weren't really any ruins. Just the bricks from the chimney, stones from the cellar, bits of metal and rock, and the edge of that cursed well. Aside from Ammi's dead horse—which they dragged off and buried—and the wagon they later returned to him, everything living was gone. The land was just five acres of dusty, gray wasteland, and nothing has grown there since. Even today, it lies open under the sky like a giant burn mark in the woods and fields. The few people brave enough to go near it call it "the blasted heath."

The stories from the area are strange. They'd be even stranger if city scientists or college researchers cared enough to test the well water or the gray dust that never seems to blow away. Plant experts should look at the stunted, twisted plants around the edge, too. Locals believe the dead land is slowly spreading—maybe an inch every year. People say the grass nearby doesn't look right in the spring. Some swear they've seen odd tracks left by wild animals in the winter snow. Snow seems lighter over that gray land, as if it doesn't settle the same. The few horses still around won't go near the valley, and hunters say their dogs act scared and unreliable near that strange patch of earth.

People also say it messes with your mind. Many folks started acting strangely after Nahum's death. Most of them never managed to leave. The stronger-willed families moved away, and only poor outsiders tried to live in the old houses. But even they couldn't stay long. Some say their strange stories about whispered spells and strange dreams come from seeing things we can't. They say the nightmares are awful in that strange land— and honestly, just looking at the place is enough to stir up creepy thoughts.

Every traveler who's passed through has felt something strange. The deep valleys are unnerving, and artists say they feel chills when painting those dark, thick woods, like there's something hidden beyond what they can see.

I still think about how I felt the one time I walked near the place—before Ammi told me his story. As the sun went down, I found myself hoping clouds would come, because looking up into the open sky made me feel weirdly afraid.

Don't ask me for answers. I don't have them. Ammi was the only person I could ask. The people in Arkham refuse to talk about those strange days, and the three professors who studied the fallen meteor and its glowing core are all gone now. But there were definitely more of those globes. One must have fed and escaped. Maybe another was too slow. I'm sure something is still down in that well—I could feel it in the way the sunlight looked above its edge.

Locals say the blight is spreading, little by little, so maybe it's still feeding and growing. Whatever that thing is, it must be stuck to something down there—otherwise, it would've taken over long ago. Maybe it's trapped in the roots of those strange trees that seem to reach and twist toward the sky. There's even a story going around Arkham about thick oak trees that glow and move at night, in ways no tree ever should.

Only God knows what it really was. If we're talking about physical matter, I guess you could call what Ammi saw some kind of gas—but it didn't behave like any gas we understand. It didn't follow the rules of nature we know. It wasn't from any planet or star that astronomers can study with telescopes or cameras. It wasn't part of the sky whose size and motion scientists can measure, or even imagine. It was just a color from space—a terrifying sign from some unfinished, unknowable place beyond everything natural. Just thinking about where it came from overwhelms the mind, opening up a black, endless void that leaves us frozen with fear.

I don't believe Ammi was lying to me on purpose, and I don't think his story was just a sign of madness, no matter what the locals said. Something awful really did arrive with that meteor—it came to the hills and valleys, and part of it, though I don't know how much, is still there. I'll be glad when the new water reservoir finally covers the place.

In the meantime, I just hope nothing bad happens to Ammi. He saw too much, and whatever that thing was, its effect on him has been slow and sneaky. I keep wondering why he's never been able to move away. He remembered Nahum's last words so clearly—"can't get away—it pulls you in—you know it's coming, but it doesn't matter—"

Ammi's a kind and gentle man. When the team starts building the reservoir, I'll make sure to write to the chief engineer and ask him to keep an eye on Ammi. I can't stand the thought of him becoming like the strange, gray, brittle figure that keeps haunting my dreams more and more.

THE END

Thank You for Reading

Dear Reader,

We hope this timeless classic has sparked your imagination and enriched your literary journey. Now that you've turned the final page, we want to share a vision for the future of reading—one where every classic you've ever wanted to explore is at your fingertips, in a format that best suits your life.

We'd like to invite you to gain immediate, unlimited digital & audiobook access to hundreds of the most treasured literary classics ever written—along with the option to secure deluxe paperback, hardcover & box set editions at printing cost. Together, we can spark a new global literary renaissance alongside our small, independent publishing house called "The Library of Alexandria."

Thousands of years ago, the Library of Alexandria stood as a beacon of knowledge—until it was lost to history. We aim to reignite that spirit of preservation and discovery right now, in the modern age—only this time, it's accessible to all, in every language and every format.

Picture a world where every timeless classic, novel, poem, or philosophical treatise is not only available to read but also updated for today's readers—modernized, translated into any language or dialect, and ready to enjoy in any format you choose, whether that is in an eBook, audiobook, paperback, or deluxe hardcover & box set version a printing cost.

By joining our movement to rebuild the modern Library of Alexandria, you become part of an unprecedented mission to offer:

- **Unlimited Audiobook & eBook Access** to the **Greatest Classics of All Time**

  Instantly explore thousands of legendary works, from Plato and Shakespeare to Jane Austen and Leo Tolstoy. All are instantly ready to read or listen to, giving you a complete literary universe at your fingertips.

- **Paperback & Deluxe Editions at Printing Costs:**

  Purchase any title in a paperback, deluxe hardbound, or deluxe boxset edition at printing costs, shipped right to your doorstep. Curate your personal library of Alexandria with editions worthy of display— crafted to last, designed to captivate, and delivered straight to your door.

- **Modern translations for Contemporary Readers in all languages and dialects**

  Discover a vast selection of classics reimagined in clear, current language—no more struggling with outdated phrases or obscure references. Next to the original versions, we aim to offer translations in as many languages and dialects as possible.

  As we continue our translation efforts and add new languages, readers everywhere can connect with these works as if they were written today. By bridging linguistic divides, you're contributing to ensuring that these timeless stories become more meaningful, accessible, and inspiring for people across the globe.

- **Your Personal Library of Alexandria:**

  Over the months and years, you'll curate a unique physical archive of classics—each volume a testament to your taste, curiosity, and love of knowledge. It's not just about owning books—it's about curating a cultural legacy you'll cherish and pass down for generations to come.

- **Join a Global Literary Renaissance:**

  Your support fuels an ongoing mission: allowing us to reinvest in offering deluxe print editions (including special boxsets) at their true cost, broaden the range of available formats and translations, and extend the reach of these works to new audiences worldwide. By joining today, you're not just preserving a legacy of masterpieces; you set in motion a powerful wave of literary accessibility.

We are more than a publisher—we're a movement, and we can't do it alone. Your support lets us scale our mission, preserving and reimagining history's greatest works for tomorrow's readers.

Become a Torchbearer of knowledge.

Thank you for picking up this book and allowing us into your literary journey. As you turn the pages, know that you're part of something larger: a global effort to keep these stories alive, share their wisdom across borders and generations, and spark a true cultural revival for the modern era.

If this resonates with you—please consider taking the next step by visiting:

www.libraryofalexandria.com

With gratitude and a shared love of knowledge,

The Modern Library of Alexandria Team

Visit:

www.libraryofalexandria.com

Or scan the code below:

www.ingramcontent.com/pod-product-compliance
Lightning Source LLC
Chambersburg PA
CBHW011525240626
47154CB00009B/2976